OLIVIA™
and the School Carnival

adapted by Tina Gallo
based on the screenplay
"OLIVIA Runs a Carnival"
written by Joe Purdy

illustrated by Guy Wolek

SIMON AND SCHUSTER

Based on the TV series OLIVIA™

First published in Great Britain in 2011 by Simon and Schuster UK Ltd
1st Floor, 222 Gray's Inn Road, London, WC1X 8HB
A CBS Company

Published in the United States by Little Simon, an imprint of Simon & Schuster Children's Publishing Division

ISBN: 978-0-85707-173-6

Printed in the United States of America

10 9 8 7 6 5 4 3 2 1

www.simonandschuster.co.uk

"In a few days, our class will be hosting parents' night," said Mrs Hoggenmuller. "Let's put our thinking caps on and come up with fun activities for the evening. Harold? Do you have any ideas?" she asked.

"We can have a finger-painting party! Only you paint with your feet!" he said.

"Thank you, Harold, I will keep that in mind," Mrs Hoggenmuller said. "Anyone else? Olivia? Do you have an idea?" Mrs Hoggenmuller asked.

"We could make our own carnival!" Olivia said. "We could have games, and rides, and prizes!"

Olivia's classmates loved her idea. And so did Mrs Hoggenmuller. "What a fantastic idea," she said. "And Olivia, I'd love for you to be in charge – with my supervision of course."

Olivia imagined what it would be like to be the ringmaster in a carnival. . .
"Step right up, everyone, and come see the best, the biggest, the most fun
carnival ever made!" Ringmaster Olivia shouted to the excited crowd.

The next day at school, Olivia placed her classmates in groups of three to make up their own booth or game for the carnival.

"How is the Ring Toss game coming along?" Olivia asked Francine's group.

"Oh sorry, Olivia," Francine said. "I decided a ring toss was too boring. So we changed it to a Pin-the-Nose-on-the-Clown game."

"I like it a lot!" Olivia said. "But what if you did something like . . ." Olivia leaned in close and whispered so only Francine could hear.

"What a great idea!" Francine said.

Next, Olivia visited Julian's group.

She stared at the brightly coloured tunnel in front of her and wondered what it was.

"We call it the Roly-Twisty Tunnel Ride," Connor explained. "Watch."

Julian crawled inside the tunnel and Connor and Daisy rolled it back and forth across the floor. When the ride was over, Julian could barely stand up straight. "I'm not so sure about this," Julian said. "It makes you kind of dizzy. Whoa." "It looks like fun to me!" Olivia said. "But it might be even MORE fun if you tried. . ." And she whispered so only Daisy, Connor, and Julian could hear. All three of them loved Olivia's idea. They couldn't wait to try it out!

Finally, Olivia checked on Harold's group. She saw a frog sitting in the middle of
a bunch of toys. "So your attraction is The World's Largest Frog?" Olivia asked.
"Yes. See how it works? He looks pretty big next to these toys," Alexandra
explained.
Before Olivia could say another word, the frog jumped and sat on Harold's head.
Harold turned and asked Alexandra, "He won't be doing that on parents' night,
will he? My mum freaks out about frogs."

"Your attraction is really great," Olivia said. "But I wonder if this might make it even better . . ." She leaned in close to whisper.

"Can you whisper your idea again?" Harold asked. "It's hard to pay attention when there's a frog on your head."

Olivia took the frog off Harold's head and whispered her suggestion right in Harold's ear. He loved it!

When class was over, Mrs Hoggenmuller spoke to Olivia. "Olivia, everyone is thrilled with your suggestions!" she said. "It looks like you're doing an excellent job as carnival director."

"Thank you, Mrs Hoggenmuller," Olivia replied.

"And how is your own special attraction coming along?" Mrs Hoggenmuller asked.

"Well, I have lots of ideas, but I haven't decided which one should be my extra special attraction," Olivia said.

Mrs Hoggenmuller smiled. "Well don't worry, dear. Great ideas have a way of sneaking up on you."

On her way home, Olivia imagined she was surrounded by reporters with microphones and cameras. . .

"Olivia, can we see your extra special, top-secret attraction now?" asks one reporter.

"Yes, Olivia, what's under the sheet?" asks another reporter.

"Only the soon-to-be most-talked-about, most-pictures-taken-of, world-famous, most amazing attraction ever built!" Olivia says.

"Show us, Olivia!" begs a third reporter.

"Sorry, but it's not ready for the public yet. You'll have to come back tomorrow, at parents' night," Olivia tells them.

That night, Olivia told her parents about her project. She showed her dad the
sketches she had made of all of her ideas.

"Okay, Dad, here's how my extra special project is going to work. . ."

Olivia's father looked at all the sketches carefully. "Hmmm, classic design, very
scientific, it pushes, it pulls . . . You just might need a little help."

Olivia's brother Ian walked into the living room. He was holding his favourite toy robot. Ian began speaking in a robotic voice.

"Why-don't-you-ask-the-boy-standing-next-to-you?" Ian asked in his best robot voice.

"Okay, you can help," Olivia said.

Ian turned to his parents. "See-you-later-parents-of-Robot-Boy."

The big night finally arrived. Mrs Hoggenmuller greeted the parents. "Welcome to parents' night!

Olivia beamed. "Thank you, Mrs Hoggenmuller! Folks, follow me to view our first attraction, which was made by Francine, Oscar, and Otto. It's the one, the only, Amazing Clown Beanbag Toss! Would someone care to try it?"

Next Olivia walked over to what used to be the Roly-Twisty Tunnel Ride. "Here we have Beach Ball Bowling," Olivia announced. "All you have to do is throw a ball through the tunnel and out the other side to knock down these bowling pins! Julian, will you demonstrate?"
Everybody cheered for Julian's strike.

Olivia walked over to the next attraction. "And step this way, ladies and gentlemen, and see The Most Strange Animal of All Time . . . the last living dinosaur, the frogosaurus! Watch it climb up a tall building!"

Harold stood behind a model of the Empire State Building and let the frogosaurus go. It hopped up the building and then right on his head again! "It's okay, Mum, it doesn't bite!" Harold said.

"And finally, for our last attraction," Olivia said, "welcome to Olivia's Spectacular Fun House!"

Olivia pointed to the fun house behind her. "I couldn't have done it without my little brother Ian!"

Ian peeked his head out from behind a flap in the fun house. "She's right, she couldn't have!"

Olivia stood in front of the fun house mirrors. "Now watch carefully as the Hall of Mirrors transforms an ordinary boy into . . . The Amazing Robot Boy!"

Ian placed his toy robot in front of the mirrors.

The mirrors made Ian's toy robot look huge! Now it looked like a real robot boy.

All the parents laughed and cheered.

Mrs Hoggenmuller walked over next to Olivia. "Great job, everyone!" she said. "Parents, enjoy the carnival!"

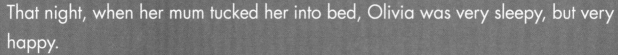

That night, when her mum tucked her into bed, Olivia was very sleepy, but very happy.

"I really want to show you my idea for a carnival booth," Olivia said.

Olivia's mum smiled. "I would love to look at your idea, Olivia . . . in the morning."

"But my idea glows in the dark, so it's really best if we talk about it now!" Olivia explained.

"Your idea will still be there in the morning. Goodnight, Olivia. Sweet dreams, honey."

"Goodnight, Mum."

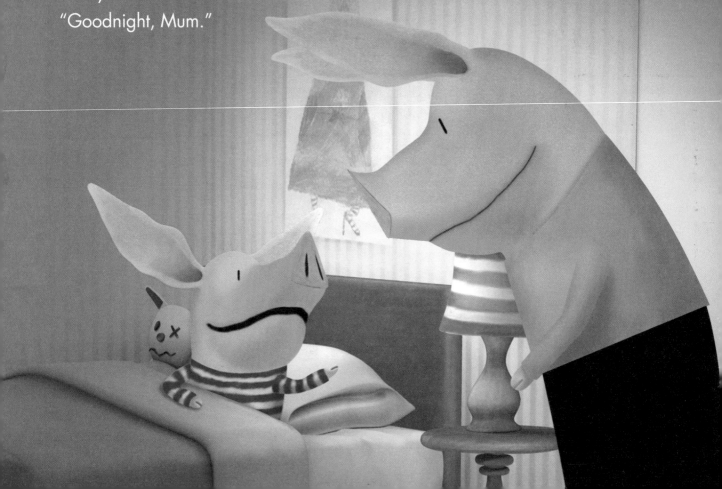